W9-BUI-747

For Uncle Jeff, Antler Amy, and Nick and Brandon Wheeler —L. W.

For Polly —B. F.

ATHENEUM BOOKS FOR YOUNG READERS ❈ An imprint of Simon & Schuster Children's Publishing Division ❈ 1230 Avenue of the Americas, New York, New York 10020 ❈ Text copyright © 2004 by Lisa Wheeler ❈ Interior illustrations copyright © 2004 by Brian Floca ❈ Jacket illustrations copyright © 2004, 2014 by Brian Floca ❈ All rights reserved, including the right of reproduction in whole or in part in any form. ❈ ATHENEUM BOOKS FOR YOUNG READERS is a registered trademark of Simon & Schuster, Inc. ❈ Atheneum logo is a trademark of Simon & Schuster, Inc. ❈ For information about special discounts for bulk purchases, please contact Simon & Schuster Special Sales at 1-866-506-1949 or business@simonandschuster.com. ❈ The Simon & Schuster Speakers Bureau can bring authors to your live event. For more information or to book an event, contact the Simon & Schuster Speakers Bureau at 1-866-248-3049 or visit our website at www.simonspeakers.com. ❈ Interior design by Polly Kanevsky ❈ The text for this book is set in Clarendon. ❈ The illustrations for this book are rendered in India ink and watercolor. ❈ Manufactured in the United States of America ❈ 0914 PCH ❈ 10 9 8 7 6 5 4 3 2 1 ❈ The Library of Congress has cataloged the hardcover edition as follows: Wheeler, Lisa, 1963– ❈ Uncles and antlers / Lisa Wheeler ; illustrated by Brian Floca.—1st ed. ❈ p. cm. ❈ "A Richard Jackson Book." ❈ Summary: Each year, all seven of Octavia's unique uncles gather from far and near to join their favorite niece in a very special job. ❈ ISBN 978-0-689-86469-8 ❈ [1. Reindeer—Fiction. 2. Uncles—Fiction. 3. Christmas—Fiction. 4. Stories in rhyme. 5. Counting.] I. Floca, Brian, ill. II. Title. ❈ PZ8.3.W5663Un 2004 ❈ [E]—dc22 2003012803 ❈ ISBN 978-1-4814-3018-0 (reissue) ❈ ISBN 978-1-4814-3568-0 (eBook)

uncles and antlers

by **lisa wheeler**

illustrated by **brian floca**

A Richard Jackson Book

Atheneum Books for Young Readers

atheneum NEW YORK LONDON TORONTO SYDNEY NEW DELHI

Seven uncles, every year,
seven uncles, travel here—
shaggy coats, scarves of red,
two tall antlers on each head.

Uncle Uno—first in line—

just flew up from Caroline,

wears lift tickets on each tine . . .

and he's my fastest uncle!

He has **one** hat.

He has **one** vest.

He wears **one** stopwatch on his chest.

He lost **one** pole. He lost **one** ski.

He says his favorite niece is ME!

THANK YOU, THANK YOU VERY MUCH,

Uncle Duce from Cameroon,

bellows out an Elvis tune.

When he sings, the girls all swoon. . . .

And he's my loudest uncle.

He has **two** wigs. He has **two** boots.

He has **two** shiny white jumpsuits.

He has **two** roadies—Gnat and Flea.

He says his favorite niece is ME!

Uncle Trey is short and wide.

Antler tines? Three on each side!

Wears a wetsuit on his hide . . .

and he's my sweetest uncle.

He has **three** masks that hide **three** chins.

He owns **three** sets of swimming fins.

We snorkel every day at **three**.

His favorite niece is—glub-glub—ME!

Uncles **one** and **two** and **three**
electrify the scenery.

Uncle Four-eyes is such fun—
brings me gifts from Galveston.
Says his antlers weigh a ton . . .
and he's my strongest uncle!

YEE-HA!

He has **four** lassos and **four** spurs.
Four-gallon hats—what he prefers!
His rope tricks are a sight to see.

He says his favorite niece is ME.

Uncle Quint is long and tall—
a star of trick-shot basketball.
He dribbled down from Montreal. . . .
And he's my coolest uncle!

WHOOSH! NOTHIN' BUT NET!

He has **five** earrings, **five** tattoos,
and **five** new pairs of brand-name shoes.
He does commercials on TV!

He
says
his
favorite
niece
is
ME.

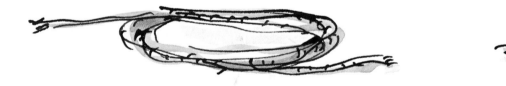

Uncle **four** and uncle **five**
wrap the gifts as snow arrives.

Here comes crazy Uncle Sy.

He's a fearless sort of guy.

Gives most any stunt a try . . .

and he's my bravest uncle!

He has **six** bumps. He has **six** scars.

He has **six** crashed-up racing cars.

He has **six** stitches on his knee.

OUCH!

He says his favorite niece is ME.

Last of all comes Uncle Sven,

a literary gentleman,

writes poetry with feathered pen . . .

and he's my smartest uncle!

Seven books and **seven** plays,

seven poems for **seven** days.

When he recites, the uncles cry.

His favorite niece? Well, it is I!

Yay for **seven**!

Yay for **six**!

They're all here now.

It's quite a mix.

Each uncle's cool!

Each uncle's great!

And I'm Octavia—number **eight**.

Eight fine reindeer, every year—
Eight fine reindeer gather here.

We do it once a year because . . .

we pull the sleigh for Santa Claus!

We change our clothes.

We hitch the sleigh.

We're ready now. . . .

We're on our way!

FREDERICK COUNTY PUBLIC LIBRARIES

JAN   2018

21982031785763

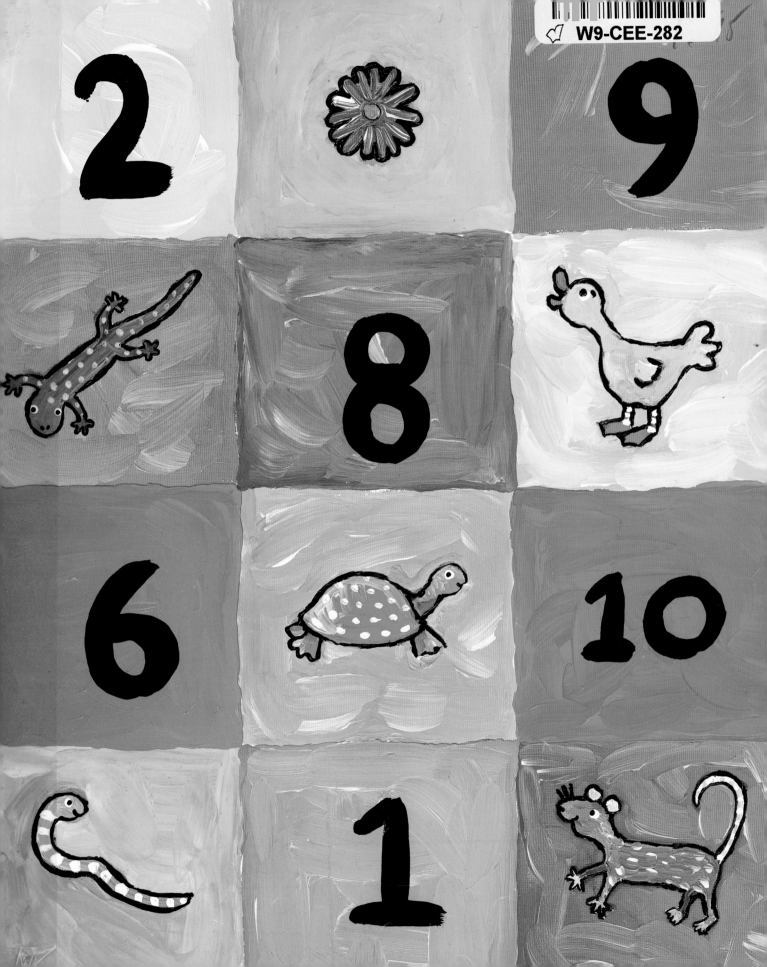

W9-CEE-282

Copyright © 1999 by Jane Cabrera
First published in Great Britain in 1999 by David & Charles Children's
Books, a division of David & Charles Limited.
First published in the United States by Holiday House, Inc., in 2000.
All Rights Reserved
Printed in Belgium
Library of Congress Cataloging-in-Publication Data
Cabrera, Jane.
     Over in the meadow / Jane Cabrera.
       p.   cm.
     Summary: A variation of the counting rhyme that introduces
   a variety of animals and their activities.
        ISBN 0-8234-1490-6
        [1. Counting. 2. Animals—Fiction. 3. Stories in rhyme.]
I. Title.
PZ8.3.C1220v 2000   99-22683
[E]—dc21   CIP

Over in the Meadow

Jane Cabrera

NO LONGER THE PROPERTY OF
BALDWIN PUBLIC LIBRARY

Holiday House / New York

BALDWIN PUBLIC LIBRARY

Over in the meadow in the sand in the sun lived Old Mother Turtle and her little turtle **one.** "Dig," said the mother. "I dig," said the one. So they dug all day in the sand in the sun.

Over in the meadow where the stream runs blue lived Old Mother Fish and her little fishes **two**. "Swim," said the mother. "We swim," said the two. So they swam all day where the stream runs blue.

Over in the meadow
in a hole in a tree
lived Old Mother Owl
and her little owls **three**.
"Tu-whoo," said the mother.
"Tu-whoo," said the three.
So they tu-whooed all day
in a hole in a tree.

Over in the meadow by the old barn door
lived Old Mother Rat and her little ratties **four**.
"Gnaw," said the mother. "We gnaw," said the four.
So they gnawed all day by the old barn door.

Over in the meadow
in a snug beehive
lived Old Mother Bee
and her little bees **five**.
"Buzz," said the mother.
"We buzz," said the five.
So they buzzed all day
in a snug beehive.

Over in the meadow in a nest made of sticks
lived Old Mother Duck and her little ducks SIX.
"Quack," said the mother. "We quack," said the six.
So they quacked all day in a nest made of sticks.

Over in the meadow in a green grass heaven lived Old Mother Frog and her little froggies **seven**. "Jump," said the mother. "We jump," said the seven. So they jumped all day in a green grass heaven.

Over in the meadow by the old, mossy gate
lived Old Mother Lizard and her little lizards **eight**.
"Bask," said the mother. "We bask," said the eight.
So they basked all day by the old, mossy gate.

Over in the meadow by the old Scotch pine
lived Old Mother Worm and her little worms **nine**.
"Wiggle," said the mother. "We wiggle," said the nine.
So they wiggled all day by the old Scotch pine.

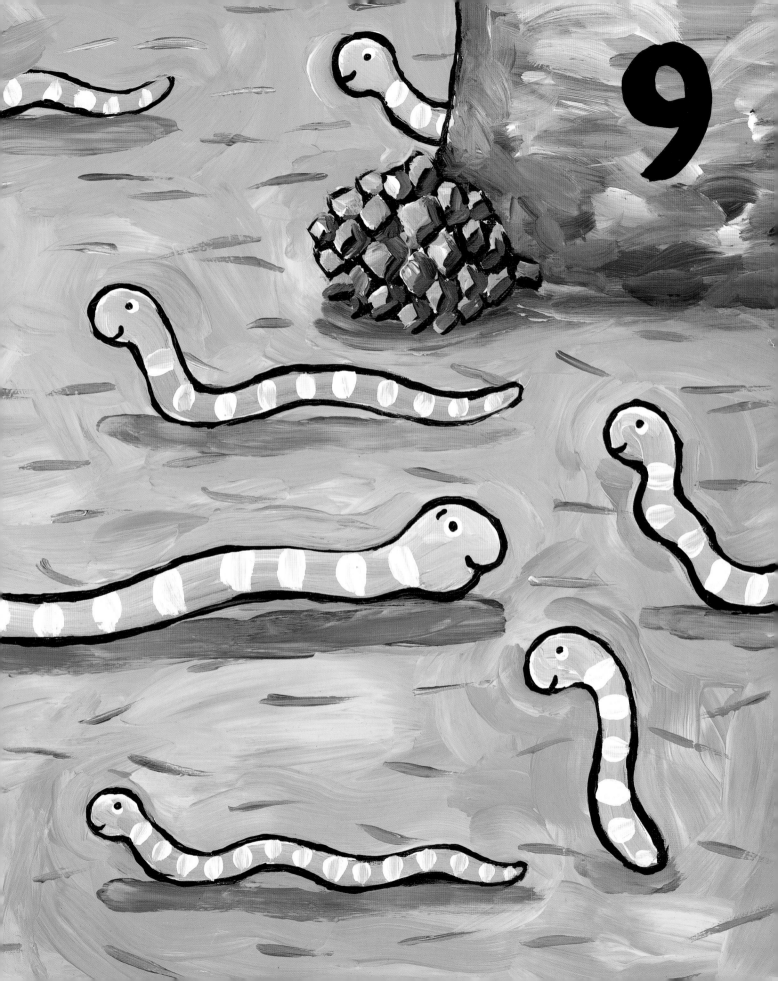

Over in the meadow
in a cozy, wee den
lived Old Mother Rabbit
and her little rabbits ten.
"Twitch," said the mother.
"We twitch," said the ten.
So they twitched all day
in a cozy, wee den.

Over in the meadow
while the mothers are away,
can you count the babies?
They've all come out to play!

One Turtle

Two Fish

Five Bees

Six Ducks

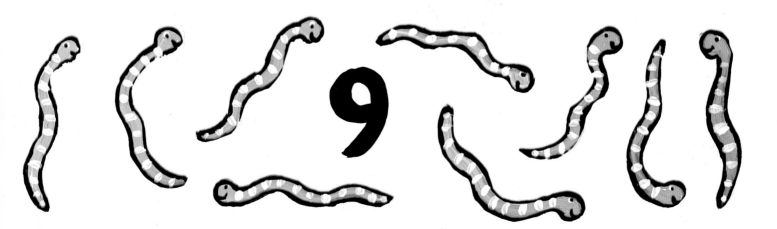

Nine Worms

3 Three Owls

4 Four Rats

7 Seven Frogs

8 Eight Lizards

10 Ten Rabbits